Pinky and Peanut:
The Adventure Begins

Pinky and Peanut:
The Adventure Begins

by

Deena Cook

and

Cherie McIntosh

Illustrated by Trina Scruggs

P & P Publishing LLC
Seattle, WA

For Denise
You are Pinky through and through and the light of my life.—Mom

For Ashley
You will always be my little peanut. My love for you is endless.—Mom

Acknowledgments

To Dennis, Chris, and all of our family and friends who helped us with this exciting adventure.

Table of Contents

The Adventure Begins

Chapter 1
Moving Stinks

"It's not fair! Why *can't* we go home?" Pinky asked her mom for the millionth time.

"Pinky, your father and I know how upsetting it was for you to leave Salem, but your father needed to take this job. This is an opportunity for us to have a wonderful life. Think of it as an adventure."

Think of it as an adventure.

How many times had Pinky's mom and dad said that over the last two months?

Pinky went out onto the front porch of their new white house and let the door slam a little bit too hard.

It had been two weeks and so far the only adventure Pinky had had in the new house was running into two huge spiders the first day they moved in.

Pinky rolled her eyes and put her head into her lap.

What kind of adventure could possibly happen in a town where she didn't know anyone and her mom and dad were so busy with their new jobs?

"Oakdale—what kind of name is Oakdale? It sounds like I live in a tree," she grumbled.

Pinky wondered why her mom and dad didn't real-ize that she had left behind all of her friends at Salem Elementary School.

Didn't they know she loved her old house in Salem?

Why did they need an adventure anyway when life had been just about perfect?

Daddy kept telling Pinky that she would make friends in a snap in second grade. He said she was his little pink fairy blossom and fairies could make friends anywhere.

That's where her nickname came from.

Pinky wasn't called Pinky when she was first born. Pinky was a special name given to her when she was a little girl.

Daddy said that when Pinky was three, she was standing under a tree of pink cherry blossoms. When the wind began to blow, a whole bunch of cherry blossoms fell into her hair. Daddy said she looked like a beautiful pink fairy standing under that tree.

Because that is what Daddy always called her, that is what everyone began to call her.

Pinky loved her nickname.

She was different, and she loved that it made her feel special. But now, who would even care about her nickname?

Would the children in second grade laugh when she told them?

Should she tell them her real name? Denise . . . Denise just didn't have the same excitement to it that Pinky did.

If no one called her Pinky, then it definitely would be an adventure—a horrible, boring, very sad adventure. She would have to think about her name a bit more. It was a good thing there were still four weeks left before second grade.

"Hmmmm," Pinky thought to herself. "How can I be happy when I feel so sad?"

Pinky twisted her wavy brown hair with her fingers. Her stomach did a flip-flop as she thought about her new life and her new school.

Just before Pinky's green eyes filled with tears, she heard a very loud noise.

"Wow, that sounds like thunder."

As she stood up to get a closer look, she spotted a large yellow moving truck coming down the road.

"Maybe they'll be as sad as I am to move to this stinky town," Pinky said to herself.

The truck stopped right across the street. Behind the truck, a blue minivan with lots of people inside came to a stop.

When Pinky took a closer look, she saw a little girl sitting in the back seat of the van.

Chapter 2
Not Fair

"**M**om, Peanut's pouting again!" shouted Scott.

"Am not!" Peanut yelled. Looking out the window of the minivan, Peanut pretended to push her blonde ponytail away from her shoulder. She hoped her brother wouldn't see the tears that were making her blue eyes red. There was no way that Peanut was going to show anyone how she really felt.

"Why doesn't he just leave me alone?" Peanut whispered to herself and glared at Scott.

Peanut still couldn't believe this was happening. She had replayed the last few weeks in her mind like a movie—a very bad movie—over and over and over again.

Her life was so fun and perfect just three weeks ago. She had friends, she loved her school, and she lived in the most beautiful house anyone had ever seen. Now her mom and dad were moving her to a place called Oakdale.

"Oakdale—what a horrible name for a town."

This just wasn't fair. Peanut's mom and dad told her she had to move because of dad's new job. They kept calling it a "great opportunity"—whatever THAT meant.

"Only four weeks left of summer," thought Peanut. "Not much time to find new friends or fun. All of my friends, my house, my school, and my favorite climbing tree are back in Highland. It's not fair!"

Peanut took out her special journal and opened it up to the next blank page. Instead of writing in her journal as she always did, this time Peanut drew a picture of herself. She made sure the face looked as sad as she felt inside.

Her journal was so important to her, but even now, it couldn't help her feel any better.

"I'll never be happy again," Peanut sighed as she looked out the minivan window.

How would this be a great opportunity?

Giving her dog a hug, she quietly whispered in his ear, "Ralphie, what if nobody likes me? What if nobody likes my name?"

Everyone always called her Peanut. What would they think? Would she have to start saying her name was Ashley again? Her nickname meant so much to her.

Mom always told Peanut that because she was the baby of the family, and she was the only girl . . . she was their own little Peanut. It made her feel special.

Would the kids think she was special or silly?

While Peanut was thinking of all the things she would miss back in Highland, someone suddenly punched her shoulder. "OWW!" Peanut cried out.

"Stop pouting; we're here!" Scott yelled loudly.

Very quietly, Peanut repeated, "We're here."

"Hey, Peanut," her older brother Paul said as he gave a gentle tug to her ponytail. "Everything will be okay, I promise."

She wanted to believe him, but she wasn't sure she could.

Peanut looked out the minivan window again and stared at the gray house with black shutters that she was about to call home. Peanut whispered, "Here goes nothing."

Peanut stepped out of the minivan and studied the street where her new *opportunity* would take place.

As Peanut walked up the path to her new house, she noticed a little girl sitting across the street on some front steps.

Guess what, Peanut thought, *she looked sad too.*

Chapter 3
The Meeting

"Stop, Ralphie! Stop now!" Peanut said with an angry face. "This crazy dog never stops for me."

It had been three days since Peanut had moved into her new house, and she didn't feel any happier. She especially didn't feel very happy that her dog kept trying to run away every time she walked him.

Peanut decided that next time she was going to have her brother Scott walk the dog.

At that moment, Ralphie began chasing a squirrel in a circle around Peanut.

"Ralphie!" screamed Peanut. "Stop right now!"

Before Peanut could finish her sentence, Ralphie had tangled the leash around her legs, making Peanut fall face first into the grass.

"Great!" yelled Peanut. "That's just great, Ralphie!"

It didn't matter what Peanut was saying though, because Ralphie had broken free and was already running across the street.

"Could my life get *any* worse?"

Still tangled in Ralphie's leash, Peanut closed her eyes and pretended for one minute that her dog had not just run away.

"Ohhh, he is so cute!"

Peanut looked up at the voice and was surprised to see the same little girl who had been sitting on her front steps across the street the day she moved in.

"I brought your dog back," the little girl said. "What's his name? I've always wanted a cute dog, and he's sooo cute!"

"His name is Ralphie."

"Ralphie—I love that name. Oh, hi, Ralphie," Pinky said as she scratched behind his ears.

Just then, Pinky realized the girl was tangled in the dog's leash.

"Looks like you had a little trouble with your dog today," Pinky said with a giggle. "Can I help you up?"

"No, I've got it, thanks," Peanut said, unwinding the leash from her legs.

"My name is Pinky."

"Your name is Pinky?" Peanut said with a laugh, dusting off the grass.

"What is so funny about my name?" Pinky said with a scowl.

"Well, it wouldn't be so funny, except my name is Peanut."

Pinky looked at Peanut, and they both burst out laughing at the same time. After that, Pinky and Peanut spent time telling each other the stories of how they got their special names.

"So, how old are you?" Pinky asked Peanut.

"I'll be eight in two months."

"Oh wow. I'm already eight," Pinky beamed.

"Oh, this is so cool! We are going to be in the same second-grade class, we both just moved here, we both like dogs, we both . . ."

"Wait a minute!" shouted Peanut. "You just moved here too?"

"I can't believe I forgot to tell you that," said Pinky. "You know what else, Peanut? Now we don't have to be

alone anymore. We'll go to second grade together. We'll be new best friends. This is going to be great!"

Peanut smiled at Pinky and bent down to pet Ralphie. She gave him a big hug and whispered in his ear, "Hey, Ralphie, maybe this won't be so bad."

Chapter 4
A Surprise

Although Peanut didn't want to admit it yet, especially to her mom and dad, she really liked her new house and backyard. The backyard was full of bright flowers and super tall trees, and it was even big enough for a pool (of course, her mom and dad laughed each time she mentioned that to them). Ralphie seemed to really like it too.

Peanut was enjoying the warm sunny day with Ralphie, throwing a ball to him.

For the first time, Peanut felt happy, really happy that her mom and dad had moved to Oakdale.

"Go, Ralphie, go!" shouted Peanut as she threw the ball over his head.

Ralphie liked to play catch more than any dog she knew. His favorite ball to play catch with was red. He'd had it since he was a puppy. It had teeth marks all over it. Yuck!

Peanut played catch for a long time with Ralphie. Her arm started to get a little sore, but Ralphie kept going. Peanut decided she was going to throw the ball one more time and then take a break.

"Let's see if you can catch this one, Ralphie!" Peanut pulled her arm back as far as she could and threw the ball at top speed.

She couldn't believe her own eyes. The ball went high into the sky and flew like a bird. Ralphie just kept running.

Peanut didn't even see where the ball dropped. She waited a little bit but still didn't see Ralphie or the ball. Peanut decided to go see what was keeping Ralphie.

As she was walking, she saw Ralphie's tail sticking out under a big cluster of bushes and trees up ahead. She ran over there, thinking Ralphie might have gotten stuck.

"Ralphie, are you okay?"

He began to bark.

Peanut pushed away the branches where she heard the barking. As she parted the branches, Peanut couldn't believe her eyes. "What in the world is this?" she said.

There in front of her was Ralphie, the red ball, and a wooden house just her size.

Peanut slowly stepped over the branches and took a closer look. The house was yellow with two windows, a blue door, and lots of spider webs all over it.

"Could I really be seeing this?" Peanut asked herself.

So many thoughts were racing through her head. She liked her backyard before she found this house. Now Peanut decided that she LOVED her backyard.

"My very own clubhouse!" Peanut shouted as she hopped in a circle on one foot.

She looked around and realized she might have been a little too loud. She didn't want her brothers to hear her—especially Scott.

She knelt down to Ralphie, gave him a kiss on the top of his head, and told him not to tell anyone.

Peanut headed back to her house. She knew exactly what to do next.

Chapter 5
So Excited

Peanut was thinking about how much fun she was having with her new best friend as she ran to Pinky's house.

For the last week and a half, they had spent every minute they could together. They rode bikes, climbed trees, had picnics, and took Ralphie for walks. Of course, Peanut never forgot to write all about it in her journal.

Peanut's mom and dad were so happy that she had made a new friend they bought the girls walkie-talkies. This way, even if they weren't together, the girls could still talk and talk and talk.

Peanut was out of breath by the time she got to the side of Pinky's house. She was SO excited.

"Hey Pinky! Pinky, can you hear me? Come to the window! Hurry!"

Pinky opened her bedroom window.

"What's up, Peanut? Whatcha yelling for?"

"Come outside quick! I've got to show you something."

Peanut could hardly wait for Pinky to put her shoes on. This secret would make this summer the BEST ever.

As soon as Pinky finished tying her shoes, Peanut grabbed her hand and made a fast dash for her backyard.

"Peanut, can't you even tell me why we're running so fast?" asked Pinky, out of breath.

"Nope!" shouted Peanut as they continued to run.

All of a sudden, Peanut just stopped. "We're here!" Peanut yelled.

"You mean we ran all the way to your house just to see your backyard," said Pinky, a little confused.

Peanut turned to Pinky and gave her a huge hug. "No, Pinky, no . . . just look!"

At that moment, Peanut pulled apart the branches and screamed, "THERE IT IS!"

"I don't get it. What do you mean? What's there?" Pinky shrugged.

"Pinky, look, really look. It's a house. This is a club-house!"

All of a sudden, Pinky's eyes opened wide. There in front of her was the little yellow house, just their size.

For a moment, no one made a sound.

"Pinky, are you okay?"

"Oh Peanut, this is GREAT—a house, a house of your very own!" Pinky began to do her best ballerina spin around the yard.

When she stopped, she noticed that Peanut was giving her a funny look.

Pinky just stood there thinking about what she had said.

"No, Pinky," Peanut said slowly, "this is OUR club-house."

"You mean it is OUR clubhouse?" Pinky asked.

Peanut nodded yes.

Pinky looked around to make sure no one else could hear.

"Hey, Peanut, does anybody else know about the secret clubhouse?"

"Nope, not even my brothers know about it," Peanut said with a giggle.

Chapter 6
The Rules

"**Y**ou know what the best part of our clubhouse is?" asked Peanut. "That no matter where we go or how many friends we will make in second grade, this is ours—all ours," said Pinky, dancing around the room with a broom.

The girls loved their new clubhouse. For the past few days, they had spent every moment fixing up the clubhouse. Pinky's mom made the cutest pink polka-dot curtains for the windows. Peanut's mom and dad bought a new rug for the inside to make it nice and cozy. The only thing left to do was the cleaning, and that was a dirty job. Between the spider webs and the dirt, the girls had a lot of work ahead of them.

"Do you know what would make this easier, Pinky? A little cleaning music."

Peanut jumped up and pressed play on her CD player. Pinky immediately threw her arms in the air and shouted, "LET'S BUST A MOVE!" The two girls were having so much fun that they didn't hear the door open.

"Hey, what are you two doing in here? What is this place?" demanded Peanut's brother Scott.

"Scott, get outta here, now!" screamed Peanut.

"I don't have to leave; you can't make me!"

"We found this first, Scott," Pinky said with her hands on her hips, making her best angry face.

Ralphie began to bark at Scott.

"See, Scott, even Ralphie agrees," Pinky said.

"What do you know? It's not even your backyard, Pinky! It's my backyard, and I'm telling my mom!" Scott turned around and ran back to the house.

"You know, Peanut, no more music; it's time for some RULES," said Pinky.

"What kind of rules?"

"The kind that keep stinky brothers out of our club-house."

Peanut took out her journal and opened it to a new page.

"Okay, Rule #1." They both thought about Rule #1. At the same time, both girls yelled, "NO BOYS AL-LOWED!"

Pinky grabbed the pen from Peanut and added, "Except for Ralphie the dog."

Pinky and Peanut laughed and laughed until their bellies hurt and they were rolling on the floor.

"Hey, Pinky," said Peanut as she tried to stop laughing, "I was thinking really hard about something last night."

"Yeah, so tell me," said Pinky as she pushed back her wavy brown hair and let out one last giggle.

"I want to leave my special journal in our clubhouse for both of us to use."

"Really?" said Pinky.

"What could be a better place to keep it than our clubhouse?"

"That is so great," said Pinky as she walked over to give Peanut a hug.

It was a good thing that Peanut had found the loose board in the floor of the clubhouse last week. What a surprise—it fit the journal perfectly.

Peanut stood up and put the journal under the board and laid the rug over the top.

A secret hiding spot for the journal—no one would know it was there except for them.

Chapter 7
More and More and More Rules

Every day, it seemed that Pinky and Peanut came up with new rules to add to the list in Peanut's special journal. While Pinky and Peanut were riding their bikes past Blueberry Lake, Peanut thought a good rule might be to use a secret handshake when they went into the club-house. Pinky thought that was a fabulous idea.

While the girls were having a picnic, Pinky came up with the rule of singing a special song before entering the clubhouse. Peanut thought that was a fabulous idea.

Each day, the girls jumped out of bed, excited to come up with new rules. Each night before bed, the girls would talk on their walkie-talkies about the new and exciting rules they came up with that day.

"Hey, Pinky, are you still awake?" Peanut whispered into the walkie-talkie one night right before bed.

"Yeah, I am, Peanut, but I'm so tired," Pinky said yawning.

"What do you think about writing all of the rules down tomorrow on a big piece of paper and taping it to one of the clubhouse walls?" Peanut asked.

"I think that would be a super idea," Pinky said with another yawn.

"Good night, Peanut."

"Good night, Pinky."

Bright and early the next morning, the girls met at the clubhouse. As Peanut was laying out the big piece of poster paper and the markers her mom had given her, Pinky walked over, lifted up the loose board, and grabbed the journal. She opened to the page where they had written all of the rules.

The girls worked hard for a long time putting together their poster.

Carefully, using their best handwriting, Pinky and Peanut wrote out their list using their very favorite color markers: pink, green, purple, and yellow. When the poster was finished, the girls taped the rules onto one wall and stood back smiling.

"You know what, Peanut? I think we did an awesome job," Pinky said with an excited giggle.

"You know what, Pinky? You're so right and this is so cool," Peanut said smiling.

Who would have guessed that two girls who were scared to move to a new city would find a best friend and have the best summer of their lives?

"I think the last thing we need to do is sign our names at the bottom and make it official," Peanut said in the most grown-up voice she could make.

Keeping a giggle in, Pinky replied, "LET'S SIGN."

They placed the journal back under the floor.

Both girls looked at the rules they had worked so hard to create.

"You know Pinky, we are so lucky," Peanut said looking around their clubhouse.

"Yeah, we are lucky."

Pinky and Peanut felt happy to have a best friend, a special clubhouse, and two more weeks of summer vacation to enjoy together.

Nothing could spoil this special summer.

The Rules

1. No Boys Allowed
   (except Ralphie the dog)

2. The Journal never leaves the Clubhouse.

3. Must know Clubhouse song and Secret handshake
   (except for Ralphie)

4. Don't let Scott hear anything we are talking about in the clubhouse!

5. Only Candy is allowed for food

6. If you make a mess clean it up within 4 days

Signed: Peanut Anne and Pinky Christine

Chapter 8
The Fight

"**W**here is it, Pinky?"

"Where's what, Peanut?"

"Where is the journal?" Peanut said with her hands on her hips.

"Why are you asking me? You know where it is."

"No, it's not there, Pinky."

"Of course it is, Peanut, and I'll show you!"

Pinky stormed over to the corner of the clubhouse where they kept the journal, but it wasn't in the secret hiding spot.

"Where'd you put the book?"

"Peanut, this is not funny," Pinky said as she whirled around and glared at Peanut.

"You should know," Peanut said with an even angrier face. "You took it!"

"I did not," Pinky said with her hands on her hips. "That's mean to say."

"I don't think I can be friends with someone who lies!" screamed Peanut.

"Well then, I guess we're not friends because you're the liar!" Pinky screamed back as she left the clubhouse and slammed the door.

Peanut sat down and wondered why Pinky had lied to her. Peanut knew it was better to find out Pinky was a liar before school started.

"Yeah, that's right," Peanut grumbled to herself. "Who needs a friend you can't trust?"

Outside, Pinky was walking home just as mad and trying to understand why her best friend would call her a liar. Why would she steal the book when the clubhouse was the best part of the summer? Pinky wiped the tears away from her green eyes and went home angry, sad, and very lonely.

Chapter 9
Nothing's Right

"This is just great!" Peanut shouted as she slammed down the milk carton on the breakfast table. When she had poured herself a glass of milk, half of it had spilled on the table. Her brothers just looked at her and didn't say a thing. Peanut went to the sink and grabbed a towel.

"Sweetheart, what's going on? Are you feeling okay?" Peanut's mom said as she put an arm on her shoulder.

"NO, I AM NOT, MOM. THIS IS ABSOLUTELY THE WORST DAY OF MY LIFE!"

Just then, Scott made a giggling sound at the table.

"That's enough, Scott," said Peanut's mom.

Peanut was so upset she ran out of the kitchen, tears streaming down her face, and went right to her room. She slammed the door and lay on her bed crying. She still couldn't understand why Pinky wasn't telling her the truth. How could her best friend in the whole wide world do this to her? Would things ever be the same again?

Peanut wiped the tears from her eyes and looked out the window. There was the clubhouse—beautiful and clean from all of their hard work. The best place in the world—until Pinky ruined it all.

Across the street, things weren't any better for Pinky. Nothing was going right for her.

When she went to brush her teeth, she squirted toothpaste all over her shirt. When she went to take out the garbage, the bag had a hole that dumped garbage all over the porch. When she went to talk to her dad, he was too busy finishing a work project. Pinky felt so alone. All she wanted to do was talk to her best friend. But did she even have a best friend anymore?

46

"I can't believe Peanut thinks I would lie," Pinky mumbled sadly to herself. "I love that clubhouse. Why would I ever take the journal?"

The last time Pinky saw it, it was in the clubhouse where it belonged. Pinky was confused, mad, and really sad.

How could this have happened?

Just then, the phone rang. Pinky's heart began to beat fast. For a minute, Pinky thought maybe it was Peanut . . . but it wasn't. Could this day get any worse?

Chapter 10
What Did
He Know?

All day long, both girls stayed at their own houses and didn't have any fun. How could they have fun when they weren't together? Even Ralphie couldn't cheer up Peanut when he jumped on her bed and gave her doggie kisses.

Just then, Peanut heard a knock on her door. She didn't want to talk to anybody, so she said, "Go away."

Her brother Paul knocked again and said, "Peanut, I want to talk to you. Please let me in."

"Oh, all right," said Peanut, "but make it quick."

Paul walked in very slowly and sat on Peanut's cozy pink chair in the corner of her room. Paul asked what was wrong.

"You wouldn't understand. It's girl stuff."

"Well, all I know, Peanut, is that you haven't been happy all day, and you haven't been any fun to be with. Sometimes when something bothers me, I feel better when I talk to someone."

Peanut looked at Paul and started to cry again. "Oh, Paul, Pinky took the special journal from our clubhouse, and she lied and said she didn't. I don't think I can ever be friends with her again."

"How do you know she took it?"

"Because we are the only two people who know about it and know where it's kept. I don't have it, so it has to be her."

"Hmmm," said Paul. "Maybe it fell or it got lost. Maybe Pinky didn't take the journal."

"Sure, take her side!" shouted Peanut.

"I am not taking any sides, Peanut, but maybe something else happened to it. It's just a thought. I gotta go,"

said Paul. "Cheer up, Peanut, everything will work out. I promise."

After Paul left Peanut's room, all she could think of was Paul saying how everything would work out. What did he know?

Chapter 11
So Sad

Peanut's mom called her for dinner. She didn't want to go, but her mom was making pasta, her very favorite.

At the dinner table, Peanut's dad asked everyone how their day had been and what they did. Peanut didn't say anything. "Peanut, how was your day, honey?" asked her dad.

"Don't ask," said Scott.

"Oh, be quiet," said Peanut.

"Okay, you two, that's enough," interrupted Mom. "Peanut and her friend Pinky are not getting along right now."

"She's not my friend," blurted Peanut.

"I'm sorry, darling," said her dad. "I'm sure it will all work out."

Peanut couldn't believe it. Why did her family keep saying that? It wasn't going to work out, not today, tomorrow, or ever. Peanut excused herself from the table and ran back to her room. She didn't want Scott to see the tears that started up again.

Things were just as bad at Pinky's house.

"Honey, I'm sure it is not as bad as what you're saying," Pinky's dad said, flipping the hamburgers on the grill.

"It is as bad as what I'm saying and even worse," Pinky grumbled.

"Well, I'm sure you girls will work something out before school begins."

"Sure, Dad," said Pinky quietly as she looked down at the ground.

"Hey, my pink fairy blossom," Pinky's dad said while lifting up her chin. "Look at me, honey. The truth always

comes out, and I promise that you and Peanut will find a way to work this out."

"Promise?" Pinky asked, looking at her dad.

"I promise," her dad replied with a smile.

"I love you, Daddy."

"I love you too, Pinky."

Chapter 12
What a Mistake

The next morning, Peanut was still in her room pouting when she heard her brothers' voices outside her door. They were talking pretty loud. Peanut walked quietly to the door, leaned until her ear was next to it, and listened to what they were saying.

"Just leave me alone," said Scott.

"I am not going to leave you alone until you tell her," said Paul.

Who are they talking about? wondered Peanut.

"Paul, bug off, you are REALLY making me mad."

"Not as mad as Mom and Dad are going to be if I go down and tell them what you did."

What is going on? Peanut thought to herself.

Finally, something else was happening that actually took her mind off of Pinky.

"All right, all right," said Scott. "You're so stupid, Paul!"

Just then, Peanut heard a knock on her door. She ran back to her bed as fast as she could and tried to act like she hadn't been listening.

When Paul opened the door, Scott came pushing through and sat down on her bed.

"Here!" he snapped. At that moment, Scott pulled something out from under his shirt and threw it on the floor.

Peanut looked down and couldn't believe what she was seeing. There was the journal from the clubhouse!

So many thoughts were going through her mind. She just kept staring at it. Could this really be their journal?

Peanut tried to talk, but nothing would come out.

"I found your journal in Scott's room, Peanut." Paul said, standing at the door. "I think Scott has something to say to you."

"Look Peanut, I just took it to be funny. I was really going to give it back," said Scott with a mean grin. "I swear."

Of course, Peanut had a hard time believing that one.

"Well, sorry you were mad today. I didn't think it was going to be such a *big* deal that I took it."

"YOU DIDN'T THINK IT WAS GOING TO BE A BIG DEAL?" shouted Peanut. "I can't even believe this. I blamed Pinky for the whole thing . . . how will she ever forgive me? She WAS telling me the truth, and I didn't believe her. Scott, you are in BIG trouble!"

Peanut ran out of her room and down the stairs yelling, "Mom, Dad, Mom, Dad!"

Oh boy, thought Scott. He knew he was really gonna get it now.

After telling her parents what happened, Peanut went slowly over to the phone, picked up the receiver, took a deep breath, and started dialing. She knew exactly what she needed to do next.

Chapter 13
Friends?

"I don't know what you want, Peanut, but I don't want to go to the clubhouse today," Pinky said with her arms crossed.

"I know, Pinky," Peanut said nervously, looking down at the porch steps. "I called and asked if I could talk to you at your house because I have something important to say."

The two girls sat quietly for a long time on Pinky's front porch.

"Well . . . if there is nothing else to say, Peanut, I am going back inside my house," Pinky said as she stood up.

"Wait, Pinky. I am so sorry."

"What?" Pinky said, slowly turning around.

"I'm sorry," Peanut said again.

Peanut told Pinky all about what Scott did and how sorry she was for not believing her.

"I am so sorry, Pinky."

All of a sudden, Pinky stood up and went into her house. Peanut felt crushed that Pinky just left her all alone on the front steps.

"I guess we're not friends anymore," Peanut said softly to herself as the first teardrop started to fall.

As Peanut stood up to go home, Pinky came out and started yelling at her from the front door.

"Hey, Peanut, where are you going?" Pinky asked.

"I get it, I get it," Peanut said, wiping her tears with the back of her hand. "I'm going home." Not only was Peanut upset, but now she was a little bit mad at Pinky for leaving her alone outside.

"That's great, Pinky, I don't need a best friend anyway!"

"I went into the house for a reason. Peanut, stop, come back!" yelled Pinky.

"Okay, so why did you go back into the house after I told you about Scott?" asked Peanut a little bit sassy.

"To get THIS, silly!" Pinky showed Peanut the bag she was holding. She grabbed Peanut's hand and sat back down on the front porch. Pinky opened the bag and pulled out the most beautiful sparkling box Peanut had ever seen. On each side of the box, there were jewels of many colors: blues, reds, greens, and purples. They sparkled every time Pinky moved the box.

Pinky asked Peanut, "Do you want to see the inside?"

All Peanut could do was nod her head yes.

Pinky slowly opened the box and Peanut saw the softest-looking purple velvet. This box looked like it belonged to a princess.

"My Grandma Nana gave me this box on my seventh birthday and told me to fill it with my wonderful memories. I've never been able to figure out what to put in my box . . . until today," Pinky said with the biggest, brightest smile Peanut had ever seen.

Chapter 14
The Keys, Please

Peanut kept staring at the beautiful new box all afternoon long.

"Are you sure you want to share your special box with me?" asked Peanut.

"Of course I do. My box says 'Memories Grow Here' and this has been the best summer of my life," said Pinky.

"Okay, Peanut, get the journal."

Pinky slowly opened the box, and Peanut put the journal inside.

It fit perfectly, just like it was meant to be there—just like Pinky and Peanut fit into their new town. What started as the worst summer of their lives became the best summer they'd ever known.

Pinky closed the box, reached into her backpack, and pulled out two keys. "This box came with two keys to keep my memories in," Pinky said handing one key to Peanut.

The keys sparkled like the jewels on the box.

"Now instead of just my memories in this box, we will have OUR memories," Pinky said to Peanut.

As Pinky went to lock the box, Peanut stopped her. "Wait Pinky, there's one more thing we need to do—one more thing."

Peanut took the journal back out again and opened it to the rules page. She wrote #7 at the bottom.

"Only the two people who have the keys may open the box of memories," Peanut said out loud as she wrote.

Pinky nodded and both girls signed the bottom of the page.

The girls realized it was getting late, and they needed to get home. Tomorrow was a big day. It was the first day

of second grade. There was so much to get ready for and not enough time.

"So, I guess I will see you at the bus stop tomorrow, Pinky."

"I'll see you at the bus stop," Pinky said with a smile.

As both girls went into their houses, they wondered to themselves what new and exciting adventures they would be able to put in their journal.

Chapter 15
Here Comes
Second Grade

As Pinky and Peanut stood outside the bus in front of Oakdale Elementary, they couldn't believe the day was finally here.

"We're really starting second grade," Pinky said, feeling like hundreds of butterflies were fluttering in her stomach.

Peanut didn't say a word. Instead, she reached into the bottom of her pocket and held her key tightly.

"Hey, are you guys just gonna stand there all day like dorks or are you gonna let the rest of us off the bus?" Scott said rudely, interrupting their happy thoughts.

"Hey, Scott," Pinky said. "GET LOST!"

Both girls stuck their tongues out at Scott and linked arms together. Not even Scott could ruin this day.

"I'm gonna tell when I get home," Scott said, running towards the school.

"Ready?" Pinky said as she looked at the school. "Ready," Peanut smiled back.

What would happen in second grade? It didn't matter—they had each other.

♡ 2nd grade is cool
      2nd grade RULES! ✿

We hope you enjoyed
Pinky and Peanut: The Adventure Begins.

Pinky and Peanut would love to hear from you.

Write to them at:
4957 Lakemont Blvd. SE
Suite C-4 #316
Bellevue, WA 98006

or

visit the girls at
www.pinkyandpeanut.com

Be on the lookout for Pinky and Peanut's second book:
Trouble Times Two

Coming soon!

Deena (Cloutier) Cook is starting a new adventure as a writer. She is a former second-grade teacher. She currently resides in Bellevue, Washington, with her husband and three children.

Cherie (Helfen) McIntosh is a first-time author of fiction books for children. She is a former kindergarten and second-grade teacher. Although she grew up in Highland, Indiana, she currently lives in Renton, Washington, with her husband and daughter.

Cherie McIntosh